The Puppies Are Here!

The Puppies Are Here!

Marc Tetro

Disney
PRESS

New York

ISBN 0-7868-3120-0 (trade); 0-7868-5047-7 (lib. bdg.)

Printed in the United States of America.

First Edition

1 3 5 7 9 10 8 6 4 2

Library of Congress Catalog Card Number: 96-83675

For all those starting a new family

—M. T.

It was love at first sight
when Pongo and Perdy met by chance
in the park one warm spring afternoon.

Soon wedding bells were ringing
and all of their friends
were invited to celebrate
along with them.

Pongo and Perdy shared their new home with
Roger and Anita and Nanny. Nanny took good
care of them all.

Before long, Pongo and Perdy decided the time was right to start a family. They were going to have puppies!

One day Perdy knew the time had come. Nanny helped Perdy while Pongo waited anxiously to see his new pups.

For Pongo it seemed to take forever.

AND THEN . . .

"THEY'RE HERE,
THE PUPPIES
ARE HERE!"

"Congratulations, Pongo,"
said Nanny.
"You're a father!
Eight puppies!

How wonderful!

"But wait, there's more!
Nine . . . ten now!

"No . . . eleven . . . twelve . . .
"thirteen . . . fourteen . . . wait a minute . . .

"Fifteen!
Fifteen puppies!
Can you imagine! ! !"

Perdy rested,
surrounded by fifteen little puppies
so small, they were
too tiny to even have their spots.

With time, the puppies got their spots—and got into trouble, too! But for Pongo and Perdy, it was a dream come true: they had a family they could call their own.

Fifteen puppies!
Can you imagine?